# The Silent Messenger

Biswajit Paria

Published by Biswajit Paria, 2024.

*To my wife Payel and daughter Titli—your love is the heartbeat of my life. This book is for you both, with all my gratitude.*

This is a work of fiction. Similarities to real people, places, or events are entirely coincidental.

THE SILENT MESSENGER

**First edition. September 28, 2024.**

Copyright © 2024 Biswajit Paria.

ISBN: 979-8224597499

Written by Biswajit Paria.

# Table of Contents

# The Silent Messenger

## Biswajit Paria

# Prologue

The wind howled through the narrow streets of Venice, carrying with it the scent of the sea and whispers from a world long forgotten. Beneath the ancient bridges, the dark waters of the canals churned under the pale glow of the moon, casting ghostly reflections against the crumbling facades of centuries-old buildings. Venice held its secrets close, buried beneath layers of history, its hidden treasures waiting to be uncovered by those daring enough to seek them.

Far from the shadows of Venice, a young girl stood on the deck of a steamboat, her wide eyes fixed on the hazy silhouette of Calcutta as it slowly came into view. Ten-year-old Isabella Rossi clutched the medallion around her neck, her fingers tracing the intricate carvings on its surface. The storm from the previous night was still fresh in her memory, its violence a stark contrast to the calm waters that now stretched before her. The journey from Italy had been long and fraught with challenges, but something about the sight of Calcutta stirred a strange mixture of excitement and unease within her.

Beside her stood her father, Major Edward Rossi, his sharp eyes scanning the horizon as if searching for something beyond the bustling docks. A high-ranking officer in the British Army, Major Rossi had always carried an air of authority and mystery. Even as a child, Isabella sensed the secrets he held—secrets that would one day unravel the careful life they had built. She had always admired her father's strength, but there was a growing darkness in his eyes, something she wasn't yet old enough to understand.

On her other side was her mother, Elena Rossi, her hand resting gently on Isabella's shoulder. Elena's love for history and culture had been the guiding light of Isabella's young life, filling her imagination with tales of ancient civilizations and lost treasures. But now, as they neared the foreign shores of Calcutta, the stories felt distant, replaced by the reality of a new world.

"Welcome to your new home," her father said, his voice devoid of emotion. Isabella could feel the weight of his words, but there was something cold, almost detached, about the way he spoke. She had felt the change in him for some time now, but the reason remained elusive. Her mother's presence was the only constant, her warmth a shield against the growing distance between them.

As the sun broke through the clouds, casting a golden light over the docks, Isabella's heart quickened. She had no way of knowing what awaited her in this foreign land—no way of predicting the events that would soon shape her life. The city before her was alive with color and chaos, its streets filled with the sounds of vendors, rickshaws, and the laughter of children. But there was something else, too. A sense of danger, of possibilities lurking beneath the surface, waiting to be uncovered.

This was the beginning of her story.

The beginning of *The Silent Messenger*.

# Chapter 1: The Silent Storm

The storm howled like a beast, rain battering the warehouse roof in relentless sheets, while thunder shook the foundations with each violent crack. Lightning flashed intermittently, casting fleeting shadows that danced along the walls, briefly revealing the derelict state of the building. Calcutta in 1942 was a city on fire—politically and literally—as the Quit India Movement sparked violent clashes between British forces and Indian freedom fighters. Amidst this chaos, another, quieter battle was about to unfold.

Detective Bijoy Chatterjee stood in the heart of the abandoned warehouse, his coat soaked through, water dripping from the brim of his hat. His sharp eyes were fixed on Isabella Rossi, just a few feet in front of him. The tension between them crackled like the storm outside, every drop of rain pounding the roof echoing the unsaid words between them.

"You've run far enough, Isabella," Bijoy said, his voice steady despite the whirlwind of emotions raging inside him. The barrel of his pistol was trained on her, unwavering. "This ends now."

Isabella stood before him, her dark hair plastered to her face, soaked through from the chase. Even now, in the middle of a storm, she looked every bit as dangerous as she was beautiful. Her eyes glinted with something between defiance and cold calculation. She had run out of moves—or so it seemed. But Isabella always had one more card to play.

"Bijoy, you know better than to think it's that simple," she replied, her voice soft but unwavering, dripping with the same dangerous allure that had drawn him in from the beginning. "You've always underestimated me."

As she spoke, Bijoy noticed the Venetian medallion around her neck glinting in the dim light—a relic of her past, of the lies she had woven. His instincts screamed at him not to listen, to stay focused, but there was something about Isabella that always blurred the lines between right and wrong.

Outside, the storm reached its peak. Inspector Satya and his men were locked in a fierce battle with Conti's smugglers, the night filled with the crack of gunfire and the relentless roar of the storm. Lightning split the sky as thunder crashed, mingling with the shouts of men and the chaos of the fight. One smuggler, drenched and desperate, lunged at Satya with a knife flashing in the lightning. Satya, ever the seasoned officer, sidestepped swiftly, twisting the man's arm with a bone-cracking snap and sending him crashing into the muddy ground.

Just as Satya regained his stance, his eyes caught the shadowy figures of Conti's men slipping through the veil of rain and darkness, heading deeper into the storm. Determined, he broke away from his group, shouting orders to cover him, and charged into the heart of the storm. The winds howled, tearing at his coat, and the rain lashed his face as the night swallowed him whole. His silhouette vanished into the swirling tempest, chasing the elusive figures of Conti's smugglers, his footsteps fading into the howling wind, leaving only the storm in his wake.

But the chaos wasn't limited to outside. As Bijoy kept his eyes on Isabella, something in his periphery caught his attention. Another flash of lightning illuminated the warehouse for a split second, revealing a smuggler hidden in the shadows, a pistol raised and aimed directly at him. In that brief moment, Bijoy's training took over. Without a second thought, he squeezed the trigger, and his bullet found its mark before the smuggler could fire. The man crumpled to the ground, the crash of thunder swallowing the sound of his fall.

Isabella didn't flinch at the gunshot, but the tension in the air thickened. She took a slow step forward, her hands raised slightly in a gesture of surrender, though her eyes told a different story. "You think this ends with me? Conti's network is far bigger than you imagine. Let me help you. Together, we can dismantle it. I can give you what you need."

Bijoy's pulse raced. He had been chasing the smuggling ring for years, but every time he got close, the leads vanished like smoke. Could Isabella really offer him the answers he sought? But he knew her too well—every word she spoke was layered with manipulation, designed to bend people to her will. Still, the temptation gnawed at him. Was it worth the risk?

"Tell me everything," Bijoy demanded, lowering his pistol only slightly. "No lies."

Isabella smiled, but it didn't reach her eyes. "Of course," she said smoothly. "I'll tell you everything."

Yet, even as she spoke, something in Bijoy's gut twisted with doubt. The storm outside seemed to grow even more ferocious, the wind howling through the cracks in the warehouse walls. Suddenly, the remaining last oil lamp lights flickered and died, plunging the warehouse into complete darkness. For a brief moment, everything went silent except for the relentless downpour outside.

And then, in the flash of a lightning bolt, Bijoy saw her—Isabella, her eyes flashing with cunning. In that split second, she made her move. Before he could react, she slipped into the shadows, vanishing into the storm as if she had never been there.

"Isabella!" Bijoy's shout was swallowed by the rain. He rushed toward the open door, but it was too late. The storm outside raged with full force, sheets of rain making it impossible to see more than a few feet ahead. She was gone.

Pluto, Bijoy's loyal companion, barked sharply at his side, as if sensing his master's frustration. Bijoy knelt down, running a hand through the dog's wet fur. "She got away," he muttered, half to himself, half to Pluto. "Again."

As he stood in the doorway, staring out into the rain-soaked darkness, the sounds of distant gunfire and sirens reminded him of the city that was still burning behind him. Isabella had escaped, but Bijoy knew this was far from over. She had slipped through his fingers once more, but somewhere out there, amidst the chaos and the storm, their paths would cross again. And next time, Bijoy swore to himself, he wouldn't let her go.

The storm slowly began to fade, but its presence lingered in the air like a ghost, much like Isabella's memory, now etched into Bijoy's mind—her face, her words, her escape. He had spared her tonight, but he knew, deep down, that their fates were now intertwined.

For now, he stood there, drenched and silent, as the storm receded into the distance and the city smoldered under a sky filled with smoke and uncertainty.

# Chapter 2: A New Life in Calcutta (1922)

The steamboat groaned as it battled the relentless waves of the Bay of Bengal. For days, it had been a treacherous journey, with the sea growing wilder with each passing hour. The heavy rain lashed against the ship's hull, and each gust of wind seemed to push the vessel closer to the abyss. The ship's whistle howled into the night, cutting through the storm as if to remind the world of its struggle to survive. The sky above was thick with dark clouds, blotting out any light from the moon and stars.

Isabella Rossi, only ten years old, lay huddled in her small bunk below deck, clutching a blanket tightly around her small frame. The cabin rocked violently with every wave, making it impossible to sleep. She could hear the creaking of the wooden walls and the occasional crash of something falling over in the darkness. Her mother, Elena Rossi, sat beside her, calmly stroking her hair, trying to comfort her daughter despite the chaos outside.

"Close your eyes, cara mia," Elena whispered, her voice as soothing as a lullaby. "The storm will pass, and soon we'll be in Calcutta. The city is waiting for us, and it will be like nothing you've ever seen."

Isabella tried to take comfort in her mother's words, but the storm outside was relentless. She could hear her father's voice booming from the deck above, shouting orders to the crew. Major Edward Rossi, a high-ranking British Army officer, was a man of iron will. Even in the face of nature's fury, he commanded respect and obedience. Isabella had always admired her father's strength, but there was something about him that had begun to unsettle her as she grew older. There were secrets he kept, things he never talked about, especially when it came to his dealings with certain men who visited their home in Italy.

The steamboat lurched again, and Isabella tightened her grip on the medallion around her neck, a gift from her mother. The medallion was beautifully engraved with a lion on one side and ancient symbols on the other. It was something Elena had given her for her birthday, a piece that carried the weight of history and stories. Her mother had always been passionate about history and artifacts, and she had passed that love down to Isabella.

"Remember the story of the lion?" Elena asked softly, smiling down at her daughter. "The lion was brave, even when the storm seemed too strong. And just like the lion, you must be brave, cara mia. Hold onto the medallion, and it will remind you of your strength."

Isabella nodded, her small fingers wrapping tightly around the medallion. Elena always had a way of making her feel safe, no matter how frightening the world outside seemed. But as the storm continued to rage, Isabella couldn't shake the sense of unease that had been growing inside her since they left Italy.

The steamboat had been their home for nearly two weeks now, carrying them across the seas from Europe to India. The journey had been long and arduous, but there had been moments of calm, when the sun had shone brightly on the ocean and the air had been warm and filled with the scent of salt. Those days felt like a distant memory now, as the storm battered the ship without mercy.

Outside the cabin, the sounds of the storm were deafening. The wind howled like a wild beast, and the rain pounded the ship with relentless force. Isabella could hear the voices of the crew shouting to one another, their words lost in the chaos. Her father's voice cut through the noise, calm and commanding, as if the storm were nothing more than an inconvenience.

"Your father is strong, just like the lion," Elena said, sensing Isabella's fear. "He will keep us safe."

Isabella wished she could believe her mother completely, but something about her father had changed in the years leading up to their journey. He had become more secretive, more distant. In Italy, men had come to their home late at night, men with hard faces and cold eyes. They would sit in her father's study, talking in low voices, their conversations full of words Isabella didn't understand—words about artifacts, shipments, and things that didn't seem to belong in the world of the British Army.

She had learned not to ask too many questions. Her father was a man of authority, and questioning him was never a good idea. But she couldn't help but wonder about the things he kept hidden, the things he never talked about.

The storm began to subside as dawn broke. The first light of day crept over the horizon, and the dark clouds slowly started to part, revealing a sky that was no longer filled with fury. The steamboat, though battered, had survived the night. Isabella let out a breath she hadn't realized she'd been holding.

By the time they reached the port of Calcutta, the sun was shining brightly. The city, with its colonial-era architecture and bustling streets, unfolded before them like a living tapestry of activity and noise. The air was thick with humidity, and the scent of spices filled the air. Isabella had never seen a place so alive, so full of energy. It was a far cry from the quiet, orderly life she had known in Italy.

"Welcome to your new home," Major Rossi said as they disembarked, his voice devoid of emotion. He was already scanning the docks, looking for the men who would greet him—men who Isabella suspected were more than just colleagues. Her father had a network of contacts that extended far beyond his role as a British Army officer, and as they stepped onto Indian soil, Isabella had the sinking feeling that her father's dealings would only grow more secretive here.

As they made their way through the crowded streets of Calcutta, Isabella's eyes widened at the sights around her. The city was a kaleidoscope of life—vendors shouting their wares, rickshaws weaving through the traffic, children running barefoot through the streets. The buildings were a mix of old colonial architecture and vibrant local structures, their walls painted in bright colors that seemed to reflect the energy of the people.

The smells were overwhelming at first—the scent of spices, incense, and street food filled the air, mixing with the earthy smell of the river that wound its way through the city. The noise was constant, a cacophony of voices, music, and the clatter of carts on cobblestones.

Isabella's heart raced as she took it all in. Calcutta was nothing like she had imagined. It was alive in a way that Italy had never been. There was a rawness to the city, a sense of possibility and danger lurking just beneath the surface.

As they made their way to their new home, Major Rossi remained silent, his eyes scanning the streets with a look of calculation. Isabella could tell that his mind was already at work, making connections, forming plans. Her father had always been a man of action, but there was something different about him now. He seemed more distant, more consumed by whatever secret world he operated in.

Their new home was a large colonial house on the outskirts of the city, surrounded by a lush garden that seemed out of place in the bustling urban environment. It was beautiful, but there was an emptiness to it, a sense of isolation that Isabella couldn't quite shake.

For the first few weeks in Calcutta, life settled into a routine. Major Rossi was rarely home, always at the barracks or off on some "official" business. Elena, on the other hand, spent her days exploring the city with Isabella, taking her to the local markets, temples, and libraries. It was during these excursions that Isabella truly began to fall in love with Calcutta. The city's rich history, its ancient temples and forgotten relics, fascinated her. And it was in these quiet moments with her mother that Isabella felt most at peace.

Elena's love for history and artifacts was infectious. She would tell Isabella stories of ancient civilizations, of lost empires and forgotten treasures. One afternoon, as they wandered through a dusty corner of their home, Elena pulled a small, worn journal from a trunk and handed it to Isabella.

"This was one of my favorite books when I was your age," Elena said with a smile. "It's full of stories about explorers and adventurers, people who traveled the world in search of history's greatest mysteries. I think you'll love it."

Isabella held the book in her hands, feeling the weight of it. The cover was faded, the pages yellowed with age, but it felt like a treasure in her hands. She knew that this book, along with the medallion her mother had given her, would become one of her most cherished possessions.

But as much as Isabella loved these moments with her mother, there was a growing sense of unease in her life. Her father's absence weighed heavily on her, and the distance between them seemed to grow with each passing day. Major Rossi was a man of few words, and when he did speak to Isabella, it was always with a cold formality that made her feel like a stranger in her own home.

The men who visited their house late at night were no longer strangers to Isabella. She recognized their faces now, their low voices carrying through the walls as they spoke to her father in his study. There was something dark about these meetings, something that made Isabella's skin crawl. She knew her father was involved in things that weren't part of his official duties, but she didn't know the full extent of it.

It wasn't until she overheard a conversation one night that the pieces began to fall into place. She had been walking past her father's study on her way to bed when she heard voices—voices that weren't speaking English or Italian. They were talking about artifacts, about shipments, about things that didn't belong in the world of the British Army.

Isabella pressed her ear to the door, her heart pounding in her chest. She knew she shouldn't be listening, but she couldn't help herself. The voices were talking about ancient artifacts, about rare treasures that were being smuggled out of the country. And her father was at the center of it all.

Her heart sank as she realized the truth. Her father wasn't just a soldier. He was a smuggler, dealing in the very things her mother had spent her life studying. The artifacts that her mother had loved and respected were nothing more than commodities to her father, objects to be bought and sold in secret deals.

Isabella didn't know what to do with this information. She felt betrayed, confused, and angry all at once. But more than anything, she felt alone. Her father was a stranger to her now, and without her mother's presence, the house felt like a prison.

As the months passed, Isabella tried to bury her feelings, throwing herself into her studies and spending more time with her mother. But the distance between her and her father continued to grow, and there was nothing she could do to bridge the gap.

And then, one day, everything changed.

Elena fell ill. It started as a simple cold, but it quickly worsened, and within weeks, she was bedridden. Isabella spent every moment she could by her mother's side, but there was nothing she could do to stop the inevitable. Elena grew weaker with each passing day, and one evening, as the sun set outside their home, she passed away, leaving Isabella alone in a world that suddenly felt much darker.

The grief was overwhelming. Isabella had lost the one person who had truly understood her, the one person who had filled her life with warmth and love. The house, once filled with her mother's laughter, now felt cold and empty.

Major Rossi didn't seem affected by his wife's death. He continued with his work as if nothing had changed, leaving Isabella to navigate her grief alone. The distance between them, once a small crack, had now become an unbridgeable chasm.

Isabella clung to the medallion her mother had given her, wearing it every day as a reminder of the love she had lost. She would sit alone in her room, reading the old storybook her mother had given her, trying to find comfort in the familiar tales of adventure and bravery. But the words felt hollow now, and no amount of stories could fill the void her mother had left behind.

# Chapter 3: Shadows and Knowledge

The death of Elena Rossi cast a long, dark shadow over the Rossi household. For Isabella, it was as though the very sun had been extinguished. Her mother had been the beacon of warmth, love, and light in her life, and now, that light was gone forever. The house, which had once echoed with Elena's laughter and gentle voice, became a cold, lonely shell.

Isabella felt as though she had lost her anchor. She was only thirteen, still a child, but the grief weighed on her like a heavy cloak. Each day seemed longer than the last, and her father's silence only deepened her isolation. Major Edward Rossi had never been an expressive man, but in the wake of Elena's death, he seemed to bury himself entirely in his work. His presence became even more fleeting, and when he was home, he was a distant figure, lost in his own world.

Isabella would retreat to her room, clutching the medallion her mother had given her and the old storybook that had been a part of her bedtime routine for as long as she could remember. The stories, once filled with adventure and magic, now felt hollow. But still, she would read them, trying to recapture some piece of the mother she had lost.

As the years passed, Isabella's grief did not fade, but she learned to live with it. She channeled her sadness into her studies, throwing herself into her academic work with a fervor that surprised even her teachers. She inherited her mother's love for history, particularly ancient civilizations and artifacts. The knowledge that had once been shared between them now became Isabella's refuge.

By the time Isabella reached her twenties, she had established herself as a rising scholar. Enrolling at the University of Calcutta, her sharp intellect and passion for history quickly caught the attention of Professor Aniruddha Ghosh, a respected authority on ancient civilizations. Professor Ghosh, who had traveled widely and conducted excavations across India and abroad, recognized something exceptional in Isabella.

"Your mind is sharp, sharper than most," Professor Aniruddha would often remark, his voice filled with approval. "You make connections where others see only scattered pieces. That's what defines a true historian."

Under his mentorship, Isabella flourished. She immersed herself in studying ancient manuscripts, mastering obscure languages, and developing a deep understanding of various historical periods. Her expertise in Venetian history, in particular, stood out—a topic that had always fascinated her due to her Italian heritage. Professor Ghosh's international network of scholars and access to rare manuscripts from across Europe gave Isabella the unique opportunity to explore the history of Venice, which was largely unknown to most scholars in Calcutta at the time.

Her proficiency in Venetian history was further fueled by her personal drive to connect with her cultural roots. With a thirst for knowledge and a desire to uncover hidden historical connections, Isabella dove into the study of Venice's past. The combination of her Italian heritage, her ability to access specialized material through Professor Ghosh's global contacts, and her relentless dedication made her an unparalleled expert in Venetian history within Calcutta's academic circles. Her growing reputation was well-deserved, and she became increasingly drawn to the academic life that had given her both purpose and recognition.

But even as she built a respectable career, another world was calling to her—the world of shadows and secrets that her father had left behind.

At twenty-five, tragedy struck Isabella's life once again when her father, Major Edward Rossi, died suddenly. His death was not accompanied by the same outpouring of grief that had followed her mother's passing. While her mother had been the heart of their family, her father had been its cold, silent leader. Isabella did not mourn him the way she had mourned Elena, but his death left a new void in her life—one that would be filled by something much darker.

With Edward Rossi gone, Isabella found herself at a crossroads. She could continue her career as a historian, follow in her mother's footsteps, and lead a life of respect and knowledge. But her father's empire—his smuggling ring, his network of powerful allies—was now hers. And though a part of her knew that this world was dangerous, she also felt an undeniable pull toward it.

Isabella had been exposed to her father's world for years, even if she had never fully understood it. She had overheard countless conversations between her father and his associates, conversations about rare artifacts, about money and power. She had seen the way men with cold, calculating eyes had come and gone from their home, carrying with them treasures that did not belong to them.

And now, those treasures were hers.

Isabella took over her father's operations with a quiet determination that surprised even her. She did not do so out of greed, but rather out of a need to assert control over her life. The world of smuggling offered her a kind of power that academia never could. It was a world where she could command respect, where she could expand her influence far beyond the walls of the University of Calcutta.

At first, she tried to keep her two lives separate. By day, she was the brilliant historian, working alongside Professor Anirudha to uncover the secrets of the past. By night, she was the heir to her father's empire, working in the shadows to move stolen artifacts across borders, negotiating deals with men who had once answered only to her father.

But keeping these worlds apart was not easy. The deeper she became involved in the smuggling ring, the more difficult it became to maintain her academic façade. And as her involvement grew, so did her relationship with the powerful Italian kingpin, **Vittorio Conti**.

Conti had been a close ally of her father's, and after Edward Rossi's death, he had reached out to Isabella. At first, their relationship was purely professional—Conti saw in Isabella the potential to carry on her father's legacy, and he was more than willing to help her expand the operation. But over time, their relationship deepened. Conti became both a mentor and a partner, teaching Isabella the intricacies of the smuggling world and helping her navigate the dangers that came with it.

Isabella was no longer just a historian. She was a player in the underworld, and with Conti's help, she began to expand her father's empire far beyond what he had ever imagined. She moved artifacts across continents, orchestrated thefts from museums and private collections, and built a network of contacts that reached from Calcutta to Venice.

The thrill of the smuggling world was intoxicating. Isabella had always been drawn to the beauty of ancient artifacts, to the stories they told of lost civilizations and forgotten histories. But now, those artifacts were more than just objects of study—they were commodities, pieces of history that could be bought and sold to the highest bidder.

And yet, there was always a part of her that remembered her mother's love for these artifacts, her reverence for history. Elena had taught Isabella to respect the past, to honor the stories that these objects carried. But her father had shown her another way—how to use those stories for power and wealth.

Isabella walked a fine line between these two worlds. By day, she was the respected scholar, delivering lectures at the University of Calcutta and gaining admiration from her peers. Professor Anirudha, unaware of her double life, praised her for her work, calling her one of the brightest minds of her generation.

But by night, she was something else entirely.

One evening, as Isabella sat in her father's old study, surrounded by the relics of his smuggling empire, she found herself thinking of her mother. She had never stopped wearing the medallion Elena had given her, and she still kept the old storybook close, though she hadn't opened it in years. The stories no longer brought her comfort, but they were a link to a world that seemed further and further away.

Her mother had been everything her father was not—warm, kind, and filled with a love for history that had shaped Isabella's own passion. And yet, it was her father's world that had claimed her in the end. She had chosen the shadows over the light, and there was no turning back now.

Isabella ran her fingers over the worn cover of the storybook, wondering what her mother would think of her now. Would Elena be proud of the historian she had become? Or would she be horrified by the empire Isabella had inherited?

The door to the study creaked open, and one of her father's old associates stepped inside, breaking her reverie. He was a man Isabella had known for years, a man who had once answered to her father but now answered to her.

"Miss Rossi," he said, his voice low and respectful. "We've received word from Venice. Conti has arranged a new shipment. The artifacts will be arriving in a week."

Isabella nodded, her mind already shifting from the past to the present. "Good. Make sure everything is in order. I don't want any mistakes."

The man bowed slightly before leaving the room, and Isabella sat back in her chair, the weight of her responsibilities pressing down on her.

This was her life now. She was no longer the little girl clutching a medallion and listening to her mother's stories. She was a woman of power, respected in both the academic world and the underworld. And though the two sides of her life seemed irreconcilable, she had found a way to make them coexist.

But deep down, Isabella knew that this balance couldn't last forever. One day, her two worlds would collide, and when they did, she would have to choose which one she truly belonged to.

For now, though, she would continue to walk the line, keeping her secrets hidden and her enemies at bay.

And all the while, the streets of Calcutta buzzed with unrest. The Quit India Movement had begun to shake the very foundations of British rule, and the city was on the verge of chaos. The British administration was struggling to maintain control, and whispers of rebellion filled the air.

In the midst of this turmoil, Isabella moved silently through the shadows, expanding her empire and securing her place in a world that was becoming increasingly dangerous. She was no longer the daughter of Major Edward Rossi—she was something more, something far more powerful.

And though she still carried her mother's medallion, a part of her wondered if she had lost the girl who had once clung to it for comfort.

# Chapter 4: The Detective's Suspicion (Early 1940s)

The early 1940s were a time of upheaval in Calcutta. The city was gripped by political unrest, with growing tensions between the British colonial government and Indian nationalists. Protests, strikes, and violent confrontations filled the streets as the demand for self-rule intensified. Amidst this turmoil, one name was steadily gaining prominence—Detective Bijoy Chatterjee. Known for his sharp intellect and methodical nature, Bijoy had become the most renowned detective in the city. His ability to connect seemingly unrelated clues had made him a legend in the world of criminal investigation.

Bijoy was rarely seen without his faithful companion, Pluto—a large, intelligent dog whose instincts often matched his master's. Pluto had saved Bijoy's life on more than one occasion, and the bond between them was unbreakable. Wherever Bijoy went, Pluto followed, alert and watchful.

While Bijoy's reputation was growing, so too was the list of enemies he had made within the city's criminal underworld. Whispers of his downfall spread among smugglers, thieves, and other nefarious figures. Among these names was Isabella Rossi.

Bijoy had heard of Isabella before their paths crossed. A respected historian, she was well-known in academic circles, particularly for her expertise in ancient Venetian manuscripts. However, there were whispers about her being involved in more than just academia—rumors of secretive dealings and connections to dangerous figures. Bijoy had filed these rumors away, but they had never fully captured his attention until the day he met her.

It was a routine visit to the University of Calcutta when Bijoy first encountered Isabella in person. He had been there to consult on another case, but the moment he saw her, he was captivated. She stood in the seminar hall, dressed in a graceful Italian gown, her dark hair flowing freely. Her beauty was striking—an effortless elegance that immediately drew Bijoy in.

But as Bijoy observed her, something gave him pause. Isabella was talking to a group of men in the back of the hall, their conversation quiet and tense. The men didn't fit in with the rest of the academic crowd—they seemed out of place, with their furtive glances and hushed tones. It was then that Bijoy's instincts kicked in. Something about the way Isabella spoke to them, her careful, low voice, made him suspicious.

The lecture she was about to deliver was on **Ancient Venetian Manuscripts**, a subject that had earned her respect in scholarly circles. As Isabella took the stage and began to speak, her voice was confident, her knowledge vast, and the audience was captivated by her words. She described the intricate details of Venetian manuscripts and their historical importance with passion. But even as Bijoy listened, he couldn't shake the feeling that something was off.

His suspicion had nothing to do with her lecture—it was the brief, hushed conversation she had with those men that lingered in his mind. Who were they? And why did their interaction seem so secretive?

When the lecture ended, Isabella was surrounded by admirers—students, professors, and academics eager to speak with her. Bijoy, however, kept his distance. He watched as she moved gracefully through the crowd, accepting praise and answering questions. But his eyes kept returning to the men she had spoken with earlier. They had disappeared from the hall as quietly as they had arrived, leaving Bijoy with more questions than answers.

In the days that followed, Bijoy couldn't stop thinking about the encounter. His curiosity had been piqued, but there was nothing concrete to go on—just a gut feeling that Isabella was involved in something deeper. Pluto, sensing his master's tension, stayed close by as Bijoy mulled over the details, silently considering the possibilities.

In the days that followed, Bijoy couldn't stop thinking about the encounter. His curiosity had been piqued, but there was nothing concrete to go on—just a gut feeling that Isabella was involved in something deeper. Pluto, sensing his master's tension, stayed close by as Bijoy mulled over the details, silently considering the possibilities. Determined to learn more, Bijoy began to investigate Isabella's past. He discovered that she had come to India at a young age with her father, Colonel Edward Rossi, a high-ranking officer in the British Army.. Although Colonel Rossi had an impeccable public record, rumors swirled beneath the surface. Whispers suggested that his position allowed him to form secretive connections with the underworld, using his influence to shield smuggling operations under the cover of British military authority. As Bijoy pieced together fragments of information, he began to suspect that Isabella might have inherited not only her father's connections but also his involvement in these illicit activities, deepening his unease about her true intentions.

It wasn't until a few days later that Bijoy's suspicions grew even stronger.

One evening, as Bijoy sat in his study, the familiar sound of knocking echoed through the quiet of his home. Pluto's ears perked up, and Bijoy knew it could only be Inspector Satya. Satya rarely sent letters—he preferred to communicate in person, especially when the matter was urgent.

Bijoy opened the door to find his old friend standing there, his expression serious.

"Satya," Bijoy greeted him, stepping aside to let him in. "What brings you here at this hour?"

Satya removed his hat, his face clouded with concern. "Something's happened at the university," he said as he entered. "Several Venetian manuscripts have gone missing from the library."

Bijoy's brow furrowed. "Missing? When did this happen?"

"Recently," Satya replied. "I've been investigating quietly, and Isabella Rossi's name has come up more than once. She's one of the few people who had access to the manuscripts."

Bijoy's mind raced. The image of Isabella speaking in hushed tones with those men came rushing back to him. Now, with the disappearance of the manuscripts, the pieces were beginning to fit together. Could Isabella be involved? Was she using her position at the university to cover up something more sinister?

"I saw her at the university," Bijoy said slowly, lighting a cigar as he often did when deep in thought. The familiar scent of tobacco filled the room. "She was speaking with some men in hushed tones. They didn't look like academics. It struck me as odd at the time, but now..."

Satya nodded. "It could be something. But we need more than just suspicion."

Bijoy leaned back in his chair, exhaling a cloud of smoke. "Isabella's careful. She's intelligent—too intelligent to make any obvious mistakes. But if she's involved in the theft of those manuscripts, there's a larger game at play here."

Satya stood, his face still serious. "Keep your eyes on her, Bijoy. If anyone can figure out what she's hiding, it's you."

After Satya left, Bijoy remained in his study, the flickering light from the lantern casting long shadows on the walls. Pluto lay by his feet, ever alert, his eyes following his master's every move. Bijoy's thoughts were filled with the possibility that Isabella was hiding something—something dangerous.

He scratched Pluto behind the ears, his mind still turning over the details. "We'll get to the bottom of this," he muttered to his loyal companion. "One way or another."

But as the night wore on, Bijoy couldn't shake the feeling that Isabella Rossi was not just another suspect—she was far more dangerous, and uncovering the truth about her might come at a cost.

# Chapter 5: The Missing Relics (1942)

The year 1942 was one of the most turbulent in Calcutta's history. The streets were alive with the roar of rebellion, and the Quit India Movement had taken hold of the city like a fever. Violence erupted at every corner—freedom fighters clashed with British forces, and the once vibrant city seemed to be suffocating under the weight of gunfire, smoke, and chaos. The air was thick with tension, the very fabric of society beginning to tear as the demand for independence grew louder.

But amidst the political upheaval, another kind of storm was brewing—a quieter, more insidious one. Far from the public eye, whispers of a grand archaeological discovery had reached the British government. Rumors spoke of an ancient site on the outskirts of Calcutta, a site that could potentially hold relics of immense historical value. What made this discovery even more tantalizing was the nature of the artifacts themselves—relics not from India, but from Venice. The Venetian civilization, with its storied history of wealth, art, and innovation, had long fascinated historians, but finding traces of it in India was unprecedented.

For the British administration, this was more than just an archaeological find—it was a chance to seize artifacts of immense value and prestige, potentially even more valuable than those found in Europe. They immediately sanctioned an excavation, placing Professor Anirudha, a respected scholar in ancient civilizations, in charge of the operation. And given her expertise in Venetian history, it was only natural that Isabella Rossi would be brought on board to assist with the excavation.

The dig site was located on the outskirts of Calcutta, near a cluster of ancient ruins that had long been forgotten by time. The area was rugged, covered in dense vegetation, and difficult to access. But as soon as the excavation began, it became clear that this was no ordinary site. Buried deep beneath layers of soil and rock were artifacts that had no place being in India—ancient Venetian coins, intricately carved statues, and fragments of what appeared to be Venetian weaponry.

Professor Anirudha, with his years of experience, was stunned. He had never encountered anything like this before. These artifacts could rewrite the history books, challenging everything historians thought they knew about the trade routes and connections between Europe and Asia during ancient times. The implications were staggering.

But while the professor was focused on the historical significance of the discovery, Isabella had other concerns. As she carefully brushed away the dirt from a gleaming Venetian medallion—similar to the one her mother had given her all those years ago—her mind raced. She knew that these artifacts were worth a fortune on the black market, and the opportunity they represented was too great to ignore.

It didn't take long for Isabella to contact her mentor, Vittorio Conti. From his base in Italy, Conti had long been involved in the smuggling of priceless artifacts, and the Venetian relics unearthed in Calcutta would be the crown jewel of his collection. Together, they hatched a plan to smuggle the artifacts out of India before the British authorities could catalog them.

Isabella played her part perfectly. To the outside world, she was the brilliant historian, working tirelessly to preserve the relics and ensure they were properly studied. But behind the scenes, she was coordinating with Conti, setting the stage for one of the most daring smuggling operations Calcutta had ever seen.

Meanwhile, Detective Bijoy Chatterjee was busy with the unrest in the city. The Quit India Movement had escalated into full-blown riots, and the British police force was stretched thin, trying to maintain control. Bijoy, ever the keen observer, had noticed the whispers of rebellion growing louder, and his instinct told him that something bigger was at play. But for now, his attention was focused on keeping order in the city, even as his mind continued to wander back to the mysterious Isabella Rossi.

Since attending her lecture, Bijoy had kept a close eye on her, though he had found little concrete evidence to confirm his suspicions. Isabella remained an enigma—a woman who moved effortlessly between the academic world and the shadowy underworld, leaving no trace of her darker activities. Bijoy knew she was involved in something illegal, but without proof, there was little he could do.

That all changed one fateful night when Inspector Satyajit, Bijoy's trusted ally, arrived at his doorstep, soaked from the evening rain. Pluto, sensing the urgency in Satyajit's demeanor, stood alert, his ears perked up as Bijoy opened the door.

"Satyajit," Bijoy greeted him, motioning for him to come inside. "What brings you here at this hour?"

Satyajit stepped into the small living room, shaking the water from his coat. "Bijoy, we have a problem. A big one."

Bijoy's eyes narrowed. "Go on."

Satyajit took a seat, his expression grim. "Artifacts—valuable Venetian artifacts—have gone missing from the University of Calcutta's vaults. They were part of the recent excavation led by Professor Anirudha."

Bijoy's heart skipped a beat. Venetian artifacts? The timing couldn't be a coincidence.

"How many artifacts are we talking about?" Bijoy asked, his voice calm despite the rush of thoughts racing through his mind.

"At least five, possibly more. The university's vault was supposed to be one of the most secure locations in the city. Only a handful of people had access to it. But somehow, someone got in and took them without a trace."

Bijoy sat back, considering the implications. If the vault had been breached, it had to be an inside job. And given the nature of the artifacts, he had a strong suspicion about who might be involved.

"Isabella Rossi," Bijoy said quietly.

Satyajit looked at him, his brow furrowed. "You think she's involved?"

Bijoy nodded slowly. "I've been watching her for a while now. There's something about her, something off. She's too well-connected, too careful. And with her expertise in Venetian history, she's the perfect candidate for something like this."

Satyajit sighed. "But we don't have any proof, do we?"

"Not yet," Bijoy admitted. "But we will. We need to start by questioning everyone who had access to the vault. And I want to speak with Professor Anirudha. He might know something, even if he doesn't realize it."

Satyajit agreed, and the two men set about planning their investigation. Bijoy knew this wouldn't be easy. Whoever had taken the artifacts had been meticulous, and if Isabella was involved, she would have covered her tracks well. But Bijoy had a reputation for solving impossible cases, and he wasn't about to let this one slip through his fingers.

The next morning, Bijoy arrived at the University of Calcutta. The campus was bustling with students and faculty, but beneath the surface, there was a palpable tension. Word of the missing artifacts had spread quickly, and the university was eager to avoid a scandal.

Bijoy made his way to Professor Anirudha's office, where he was greeted by the sight of the elderly professor hunched over a collection of ancient scrolls. Anirudha looked up as Bijoy entered, adjusting his glasses as he recognized the detective.

"Detective Chatterjee," the professor greeted him with a warm smile. "To what do I owe the pleasure?"

Bijoy wasted no time. "I'm here about the missing artifacts, Professor."

Anirudha's smile faded. He leaned back in his chair, his expression troubled. "Yes, I heard about that. A terrible loss. Those relics were priceless."

"Do you have any idea who might have taken them?" Bijoy asked, his tone measured.

The professor shook his head. "I'm afraid not. I was under the impression that the vault was secure. Only a few of us had access to it."

"And who are those few?" Bijoy pressed.

Anirudha hesitated for a moment before responding. "Myself, of course. A few other members of the faculty. And... Isabella Rossi."

Bijoy's eyes locked onto the professor's. "Isabella had access?"

"Yes," Anirudha confirmed. "She's been invaluable in helping with the excavation. Her knowledge of Venetian history is unparalleled."

Bijoy nodded, his suspicions growing. "And have you noticed anything unusual about her lately? Any changes in behavior?"

The professor seemed puzzled by the question. "No, not at all. She's as dedicated as ever. Why do you ask?"

Bijoy didn't answer immediately. He could sense that the professor was genuinely unaware of Isabella's possible involvement, and there was no point in alarming him just yet.

"Just covering all the bases, Professor," Bijoy said finally. "Thank you for your time."

As Bijoy left the office, he couldn't shake the feeling that Isabella was at the center of this. The missing artifacts, her involvement in the excavation, her connections to the underworld—it all pointed to her. But proving it would be another matter entirely.

That night, as the rain poured down over Calcutta, Bijoy sat in his small home, going over the details of the case. Pluto lay at his feet, occasionally lifting his head to glance at his master. Bijoy's mind was racing. He knew he was close, but without concrete evidence, Isabella would slip away once again.

Then, as if on cue, the door creaked open, and Satyajit stepped inside, his face grim.

"Bijoy," he said, "we've got another problem. One of your informants has been found dead. Murdered. And I don't think it's a coincidence."

Bijoy's heart sank. The stakes were getting higher.

Whoever was behind this wasn't just stealing artifacts—they were willing to kill to keep their secrets.

Bijoy stood, his hand resting on Pluto's head. "We need to move quickly, Satyajit. If we don't catch them soon, more people are going to die."

And with that, the hunt for the missing relics—and for Isabella—was officially on.

# Chapter 6: Letters from the Shadows

The monsoon rains came to Calcutta with a vengeance, as if the heavens themselves were trying to cleanse the city of its sins. But the downpour did little to wash away the darkness that had settled in the streets. The political unrest caused by the Quit India Movement only grew more intense, and the city remained on the brink of chaos. The air was thick with tension, the sound of gunfire and protests blending with the relentless drumming of rain on the cobblestones.

Bijoy Chatterjee had never felt so burdened. In his years as a detective, he had solved countless cases, uncovered numerous secrets, and brought justice to those who deserved it. But now, things felt different. Calcutta had always been a city full of intrigue and mystery, but the web he now found himself tangled in was more complex than anything he had ever encountered before. The missing Venetian artifacts, the underworld's growing influence, and the mysterious figure of Isabella Rossi haunted his thoughts.

Sitting at his desk late one evening, Bijoy absentmindedly twirled the handle of his pistol while Pluto, his loyal dog, lay at his feet. The room was dimly lit by a flickering oil lamp, casting long shadows on the walls. The storm outside roared like an angry beast, the wind rattling the windows and making it hard to focus.

It was then that he heard it—a soft knock on the door. Bijoy's hand instinctively moved to his pistol, but Pluto had already risen, alert and growling low in his throat. The detective walked cautiously to the door, pistol at the ready, and swung it open. But instead of a person, there was only an envelope. A plain, unmarked envelope, now slightly damp from the rain, lay at his doorstep.

Pluto sniffed at the envelope but showed no signs of concern. Bijoy picked it up, turning it over in his hands before tearing it open. Inside was a single sheet of paper, with handwriting that was elegant yet cold. The words sent a chill down his spine:

**"One will die tomorrow, Bijoy. Can you stop it?"**

No signature. No clues as to who might have sent it. Just a taunt—a dare.

Bijoy's mind raced. A murder? Tomorrow? Who? Where? And why was he being warned? He had no time to waste. With a sense of urgency, he grabbed his coat and hat, whistled for Pluto, and headed out into the rain-soaked night.

The next day, the body was found. A man in his thirties, an accountant who had no known enemies, had been stabbed to death in his home. Bijoy had arrived too late, the taunting letter still fresh in his mind. He cursed himself for not acting faster, for not piecing together the clues that might have saved the man's life.

But as he examined the crime scene, something struck him as odd. The murder, brutal as it was, didn't seem connected to any of the cases he had been working on. It felt random, almost... staged. The same thought nagged at him for the rest of the day. This wasn't just a murder; it was a message. Someone was toying with him, trying to distract him.

Then, two days later, another letter arrived. This time it was more direct, the handwriting the same as before:

**"Another will die tomorrow, Bijoy. Can you stop it? Or will you fail again?"**

The taunts burned in his mind. Whoever was sending these letters was watching him, playing with him like a puppet on strings. The murders were a distraction—he was certain of it now. But from what?

It didn't take long for the answer to reveal itself. Bijoy had been so consumed by the letters and the murders that he had lost sight of the bigger picture—the missing Venetian artifacts. In his gut, he knew that the two were connected. Someone was trying to keep him off the trail of the smuggling operation, trying to make sure he was too busy solving murders to notice what was happening right under his nose.

And the more he thought about it, the more convinced he became that the person behind it all was Isabella Rossi.

Isabella was no stranger to deception. She had been raised in a world where secrets and lies were currency, where one's survival depended on staying two steps ahead of everyone else. Since her father's death, she had carefully expanded the smuggling empire he had built, growing it into something formidable. And now, under the command of her mentor Vittorio Conti, she was about to pull off one of her most ambitious operations yet—the smuggling of the priceless Venetian artifacts out of India and into the hands of wealthy collectors across Europe.

Isabella knew that Bijoy Chatterjee was a threat. His reputation as a detective was well-earned, and she had seen firsthand how dangerous his intelligence could be. Their previous encounters had left her both intrigued and wary of him. Bijoy was a man of principle, someone who could not be bought or swayed. But that didn't mean he couldn't be distracted.

The letters had been her idea, a way to keep Bijoy off her trail while she worked behind the scenes to ensure that the artifacts made their way safely out of Calcutta. It was a dangerous game, but Isabella thrived on danger. She had grown accustomed to walking the line between respectability and criminality, and the thrill of outwitting someone as sharp as Bijoy only added to the excitement.

She knew that Bijoy would try to solve the murders. He was too proud, too determined to let them go unsolved. And while he was chasing ghosts, she would be able to finalize the smuggling operation without interference.

But Bijoy wasn't a man who gave up easily. Even as the murders continued, he couldn't shake the feeling that the letters were part of a larger scheme. He had been distracted, yes, but now he was beginning to see the pattern. The murders were too random, too disconnected from anything significant. And the fact that the letters were being sent directly to him was the biggest clue of all—someone wanted him distracted, and that someone had to be connected to the missing artifacts.

He began to dig deeper into Isabella's background. Her involvement in the excavation of the Venetian artifacts was no secret, but her connections to the underworld were harder to trace. Still, Bijoy had his sources, and slowly, piece by piece, he began to uncover the truth.

Isabella's relationship with Vittorio Conti had been carefully hidden, but not carefully enough. Bijoy found documents linking Conti to several recent smuggling operations in Europe, and there were whispers that Conti's network extended all the way to India. The more Bijoy learned, the more convinced he became that Isabella was the key to unraveling the entire operation.

But proving it was another matter. Isabella was clever—too clever to leave any obvious trail. And Bijoy knew that if he confronted her without solid evidence, she would slip away, just as she had before.

The letters continued to arrive, each one detailing another murder, each one daring Bijoy to stop it. And each time, Bijoy found himself racing against the clock, trying to prevent the inevitable. But no matter how hard he tried, he always arrived too late. The frustration gnawed at him, and the weight of the murders hung heavy on his conscience.

But as the murders mounted, so did Bijoy's resolve. He knew that the only way to stop the killings was to get to the source of the letters. And the more he investigated, the more certain he became that Isabella was behind them. The timing, the precision, the way the letters distracted him just when the smuggling operation was reaching its peak—it all pointed to her.

Bijoy's suspicions were confirmed one night when he received a tip from one of his informants—a low-level smuggler who had once worked for Conti. The informant claimed to have seen Isabella meeting with Conti's men at a warehouse near the docks.

Bijoy knew this was it—the break he had been waiting for. Armed with the informant's information and his own growing suspicion, he prepared to confront Isabella once and for all. The letters, the murders, the missing artifacts—it all led back to her.

As the storm raged outside, Bijoy stood by the window, staring out at the rain-soaked streets of Calcutta. Pluto sat at his feet, sensing his master's tension. Bijoy's mind was racing, the pieces of the puzzle finally coming together. He had been played, distracted by the letters and the murders, but now he saw the truth clearly.

Isabella Rossi was at the heart of it all. And soon, she would face justice.

# Chapter 7: The Warehouse Showdown

The storm over Calcutta continued its relentless assault, a swirling vortex of wind and rain that transformed the city into a battleground. In 1942, Calcutta was caught in the grip of both nature's fury and the political unrest of the Quit India Movement. The chaos of protests and riots raged in the streets, but tonight, a quieter, more personal conflict was about to reach its climax in the darkened corners of an old warehouse by the docks.

Detective Bijoy Chatterjee and Inspector Satya trudged through the deluge, their coats soaked, faces grim, and hearts determined. The storm mirrored the turmoil inside them—both men knew this would be the final confrontation. The stolen Venetian artifacts, the heart of the international smuggling operation, lay hidden inside the warehouse, and Isabella Rossi, the enigmatic woman at the center of it all, was somewhere in the shadows, waiting.

Bijoy's face was a mask of cold determination. He had pursued Isabella for years, always one step behind her, always chasing after the woman who had slipped through his fingers time and time again. But tonight, things would be different.

As they neared the warehouse, the flicker of oil lamps offered faint light in the black night. The wind howled like a beast, tearing at their clothes, and Pluto, Bijoy's loyal dog, moved beside him, his ears pricked, sensing the danger.

"Let's do this," Satya muttered, his voice barely audible over the howling storm. His grip on his revolver tightened as he moved toward the side of the building.

Satya crouched low, moving swiftly through the rain-soaked darkness. His eyes locked on a smuggler fumbling with a cigarette, his hand trembling as he tried to light it in the rain. Without making a sound, Satya crept up behind him, grabbed the man's arm, and with a quick twist, knocked him unconscious against the side of a crate.

But the sound of the scuffle had alerted the others. Two more smugglers appeared, guns drawn. Satya dove behind a stack of crates just as bullets whizzed past his head. The storm swallowed the sound of the shots, turning them into nothing more than dull thuds against the pounding rain.

Satya returned fire, hitting one smuggler square in the chest. The man crumpled to the ground, his body limp. The other smuggler fired wildly into the dark, panic etched on his face. Satya wasted no time, his second shot dropping the man where he stood.

He wiped the rain from his face, his eyes narrowing as more shadows moved in the distance—Conti's men, retreating deeper into the storm. Satya gave chase, disappearing into the night, the storm swallowing him whole.

Inside the warehouse, the atmosphere was oppressive. The sound of the storm outside echoed through the cavernous space, the wind howling through cracks in the walls. The air was thick with the smell of damp wood, seawater, and something else—fear. Crates filled with stolen relics were stacked haphazardly, their contents worth millions on the black market.

Bijoy moved cautiously through the rows of crates, his pistol drawn. The flicker of the oil lamps cast long, eerie shadows across the floor. Somewhere in the darkness, Isabella was hiding, waiting for the right moment to strike.

Suddenly, a shot rang out.

The bullet whizzed past Bijoy's head, embedding itself in the wooden crate beside him. He dropped to the ground instinctively, rolling behind a stack of crates. His heart raced, his mind sharp. Isabella was close, but she wasn't going to reveal herself. She was lurking, using the darkness and the storm to her advantage, just as she always had.

Another shot echoed through the warehouse, but Bijoy was ready this time. He moved quickly, avoiding the bullet as it ricocheted off a metal beam above him. Isabella was hidden, somewhere in the shadows, firing from cover. Bijoy's senses were on high alert, every nerve in his body tense as he scanned the area for any sign of her.

The storm outside roared louder, the wind hammering the metal roof as if it would tear the warehouse apart. The flickering light from the lamps barely illuminated the rows of crates, but Bijoy's eyes were trained for movement.

Another shot—this one grazed his arm, sending a sharp pain radiating through his body. Bijoy gritted his teeth, clutching his wound as he ducked behind another crate. She had wounded him, but she hadn't won yet.

Then, in a brief flash of lightning, Bijoy caught a glimpse of her—a shadow moving swiftly between the crates. He raised his pistol, aiming for the space where he had seen the movement. He fired, the sound of the gunshot swallowed by the storm. There was no scream, no sound to indicate he had hit his mark, but he moved forward cautiously, his eyes narrowing as he approached the area.

Bijoy rounded the corner, his pistol aimed and ready. There, slumped against a stack of crates, was Isabella. Her gun lay a few feet away, her hand clutching her side where blood seeped through her dress. She had been hit, but not fatally.

For a moment, time seemed to slow. The storm raged outside, the rain hammering against the roof, but inside the warehouse, everything was still. Isabella's eyes met Bijoy's, her face pale but defiant. She was wounded, cornered, but not broken.

"It's over, Isabella," Bijoy said, his voice steady despite the adrenaline coursing through his veins. He kept his pistol trained on her, his finger resting on the trigger.

Isabella's breath came in shallow gasps as she leaned against the crates. "Bijoy..." she whispered, her voice trembling. "Please... don't do this."

Bijoy's jaw clenched. He had waited for this moment for years, had chased her across continents, through lies and betrayals, and now she was finally within his grasp. But something about the way she said his name made him hesitate.

"I can help you," Isabella continued, her voice soft but desperate. "I know everything about Conti's network. Let me live, and I'll give you what you need."

Bijoy's heart pounded in his chest. He had her. After all these years, after all the times she had slipped through his fingers, she was finally here. But could he trust her? Could he believe anything she said?

"Tell me everything," Bijoy demanded, lowering his pistol only slightly. "No lies."

Isabella gave a weak smile, but it didn't reach her eyes. "Of course," she said, her voice barely above a whisper. "I'll tell you everything."

Even as she spoke, Bijoy's gut twisted with doubt. The storm outside seemed to grow even more ferocious, the wind howling like a beast through the cracks in the walls. The oil lamp above them flickered weakly, casting erratic shadows across Isabella's face. Bijoy's grip tightened on his pistol.

And then, the last flickering light went out.

The warehouse was plunged into complete darkness. For a brief moment, the world was silent except for the relentless downpour outside. Bijoy's pulse quickened as he strained to see through the darkness, his body tense, every muscle ready to spring into action.

Then, in the flash of lightning, he saw her—Isabella, her eyes flashing with cunning. She had been playing him. In that split second, she made her move, her body slipping into the shadows like a ghost.

"Isabella!" Bijoy shouted, his voice lost to the storm. He fired a shot into the darkness, but it was too late. She was gone, vanished into the stormy night like smoke on the wind.

Bijoy rushed toward the open door, but the sheets of rain and howling wind made it impossible to see more than a few feet ahead. He stood there, panting, the storm lashing at his face, as he realized she had escaped.

Pluto barked sharply at his side, sensing his master's frustration. Bijoy knelt down, running a hand through the dog's wet fur. "She got away," he muttered, half to himself, half to Pluto. "Again."

Satya returned moments later, his coat soaked through, his face grim as he approached Bijoy. "She's gone?" he asked, already knowing the answer.

Bijoy nodded, his gaze fixed on the storm. "She escaped. But this isn't over."

Satya sighed, wiping the rain from his face. "We'll find her again," he said. "We always do."

The storm began to recede, its fury ebbing as the night wore on. Bijoy stood in the doorway of the warehouse, staring out into the rain-soaked darkness, his thoughts consumed by Isabella's escape.

She had slipped through his fingers once more, but he knew, deep down, that this wasn't the end.

Somewhere out there, amidst the chaos and the storm, Isabella was waiting. And when the time came, their paths would cross again.

For now, Bijoy stood alone, drenched and silent, as the storm slowly faded into the distance, leaving the city smoldering under a sky filled with smoke and uncertainty.

# Chapter 8: The Cairo Encounter

The scorching heat of Cairo was unlike anything Bijoy Chatterjee had ever experienced. The bustling streets were alive with the sounds of traders bartering, camels plodding through the crowds, and the distant hum of the desert wind. But Bijoy wasn't here for the wonders of the city. He had traveled across continents for a reason, a name that had haunted him for years—Isabella Rossi.

Since the stormy night in Calcutta, when she vanished into the rain-soaked darkness, Bijoy had never been able to shake the feeling that their story wasn't over. And now, after years of silence, he had finally received solid intelligence: Isabella had resurfaced in Cairo. Not only had she escaped from his grasp, but she had rebuilt her smuggling empire, stronger than ever. Rumor had it she was the queen of a new underworld, pulling the strings behind the scenes, controlling a vast network of illicit trade. But she wasn't the only one with power in Cairo.

As Bijoy dug deeper into the city's criminal underworld, another name kept cropping up—Rahim al-Zahir. A ruthless warlord with a tight grip on Cairo's smuggling operations, Rahim had made it clear that no one could challenge his dominance. And yet, Isabella was doing just that. Tensions between her and Rahim were high, and clashes between their men were becoming more frequent. It was clear to Bijoy that Rahim was not just a threat to Isabella's empire but to her life. Yet, as much as Bijoy wanted to bring her to justice, he couldn't shake the feeling that something bigger was at play here.

One evening, after weeks of searching, Bijoy found himself wandering near the Grand Mosque. The sun had dipped below the horizon, and the desert wind had picked up, swirling through the narrow streets of Cairo. The call to prayer echoed in the air as men in robes made their way toward the mosque. Bijoy moved quietly through the crowd, his eyes sharp, his instincts telling him that something was off.

He spotted them—a group of men huddled together, speaking in hushed tones, casting furtive glances around them. Something about their posture, the way they moved, made the hairs on the back of Bijoy's neck stand up. He knew trouble when he saw it, and these men were trouble. As they dispersed and made their way into the courtyard of the mosque, Bijoy followed, keeping his distance but never losing sight of them.

His instincts were right. Inside the courtyard, a woman in a flowing black burkha was moving toward the entrance of the mosque. The men closed in on her. Bijoy's heart quickened as he realized what was about to happen. Without thinking, he pushed through the crowd, his hand instinctively going to the gun holstered at his side. He couldn't let them harm her, even if he didn't know who she was.

The men attacked swiftly, but Bijoy was faster. He grabbed the first one, slamming him into a wall, and pulled his gun, firing a warning shot that sent the others scrambling. Chaos erupted as the crowd panicked, but Bijoy didn't let up. He moved with precision, taking down the attackers one by one until only their groans of pain remained in the air. The fight was over.

Bijoy turned his attention to the woman, who had collapsed to the ground during the struggle. Her burkha had fallen slightly, revealing a glimpse of her face. He knelt beside her, his heart still pounding from the adrenaline of the fight. Gently, he lifted the veil, and his breath caught in his throat.

It was Isabella.

Her face was pale, her eyes fluttering as she struggled to stay conscious. Bijoy could hardly believe what he was seeing. After all these years, here she was, lying in his arms, vulnerable in a way he had never imagined. For a brief moment, he was frozen, caught between the memories of their last encounter and the reality of the woman before him.

Isabella stirred, her eyelids flickering open as she tried to focus on the man above her. When her gaze finally locked onto his, her eyes widened in shock. "Bijoy?" Her voice was barely a whisper, but the disbelief was clear.

"Yes, Isabella," he replied, his voice thick with emotion he hadn't expected to feel. "It's me."

Isabella tried to sit up, but the effort was too much. She slumped back, her strength fading. Without thinking, Bijoy scooped her into his arms and carried her through the winding streets of Cairo, his mind racing with questions. What had she gotten herself into? And why did he still feel the need to protect her, after everything she had done?

Bijoy took Isabella back to the small cottage he had rented on the outskirts of the city, away from the prying eyes of the underworld. He laid her gently on the bed, and for the next few hours, he watched over her as she slowly recovered from the shock. As night fell, the desert wind howled outside, but inside, there was only silence—broken occasionally by Isabella's soft breaths as she slept.

When she finally woke, the room was dimly lit by a single lantern. Isabella blinked, her mind still foggy, but the moment her eyes landed on Bijoy, the memories came flooding back.

"You saved me," she whispered, her voice weak but filled with surprise.

Bijoy's jaw tightened. "I didn't know it was you."

A silence fell between them, heavy with unspoken words. Isabella sat up slowly, her hand instinctively reaching for the medallion she always wore around her neck. It was a gesture Bijoy remembered all too well.

"What are you doing here, Bijoy?" she asked, her voice steadying.

"I came for you," he said bluntly. "To bring you to justice."

Isabella's eyes darkened. "You still think you can stop me?"

Bijoy leaned forward, his gaze intense. "I should have stopped you in Calcutta. I won't make the same mistake again."

For a moment, Isabella's face was unreadable, but then her lips curled into a bitter smile. "You have no idea what's happening here, do you?"

Bijoy's brow furrowed. "I know enough."

Isabella shook her head, her expression softening slightly. "Rahim al-Zahir is more dangerous than you can imagine. He's not just after my empire—he wants me dead. And now that you've interfered, he'll come after you too."

Bijoy's eyes narrowed. "I can handle Rahim."

Isabella let out a soft, humorless laugh. "You don't understand. Rahim controls half of Cairo. His men are everywhere. He won't stop until he has everything I've built—and he won't think twice about killing anyone who stands in his way."

Bijoy stood, pacing the small room. He had heard of Rahim al-Zahir, but he hadn't realized the extent of the threat. If what Isabella said was true, then they were both in grave danger.

"And what about you?" Bijoy asked, turning to face her. "Are you just going to keep running?"

Isabella met his gaze, her expression hardening. "I'm not running, Bijoy. I'm fighting. But I can't do it alone."

Bijoy paused, considering her words. It wasn't just about bringing Isabella to justice anymore. If Rahim was as powerful as she claimed, then they were both in over their heads. He had come to Cairo to stop her, but now he was beginning to see that they had a common enemy.

"What's your plan?" Bijoy asked, his voice low.

Isabella hesitated for a moment before replying. "We take Rahim down. Together."

Bijoy's jaw tightened. "And then what?"

Isabella's gaze softened, a flicker of vulnerability crossing her face. "Then I leave. For good."

Bijoy stared at her, weighing his options. He didn't trust her—how could he, after everything that had happened? But he couldn't deny that they were stronger together than apart. If they stood any chance of defeating Rahim, they would need to work together.

Finally, Bijoy nodded. "We take him down. But once this is over, we settle our score."

Isabella's eyes flickered with something unreadable—gratitude, perhaps, or maybe regret. "Deal," she said softly.

And so, the unlikely alliance was forged. Together, they would face Rahim al-Zahir and his army, fighting side by side in the streets of Cairo. But even as they prepared for the battle ahead, Bijoy couldn't shake the feeling that this was only the beginning.

As the desert wind howled outside the small cottage, Bijoy glanced at Isabella, who sat quietly by the window, her face illuminated by the soft glow of the lantern. For all their differences, there was a strange connection between them—one that neither could deny.

In the days that followed, Bijoy and Isabella worked tirelessly to gather information on Rahim's operations. They fought in the shadows, taking down Rahim's men one by one, but it soon became clear that they couldn't defeat him alone. Rahim's power was too great, his reach too wide. Every time they thought they had the upper hand, Rahim's men struck back, leaving them battered and bruised.

But through it all, something unexpected began to happen. The tension that had once defined their relationship started to fade, replaced by a growing respect for each other's strengths. Isabella was no longer the enemy Bijoy had once believed her to be. She was a fighter, just like him, trying to survive in a world that sought to destroy her.

Onenight, after barely escaping an ambush, they found themselves alone in a safe house, the flickering light of a candle casting shadows on the walls. The exhaustion from the day's battle hung in the air, but so did something else—an unspoken tension that neither could ignore.

"You're not what I expected," Isabella said quietly, her eyes meeting his across the room.

Bijoy looked at her, his heart pounding in his chest. "And you're not who I thought you were."

There was a long silence between them, the kind of silence that was filled with meaning, with all the things they wanted to say but couldn't. And then, without warning, the distance between them seemed to disappear.

As their lips met in a soft, unexpected kiss, Bijoy knew that their story was far from over.

# Chapter 9: Unlikely Allies

The streets of Cairo had become a battlefield. Every corner held a threat, every alley whispered danger, and Bijoy and Isabella were caught in the heart of it all. Their alliance, though born out of necessity, had grown into something deeper. Together, they fought side by side, their movements synchronized, their instincts sharp. Rahim al-Zahir's forces had underestimated them at first, but now they were closing in.

With each day, they dismantled more of Rahim's operations. Bijoy, with his sharp mind and relentless pursuit, and Isabella, with her cunning and intimate knowledge of the underworld, made an unstoppable team. Rahim's men fell one by one, their smuggling routes disrupted, their strongholds taken down. Yet, as they delved deeper into Rahim's network, they realized that his grip on Cairo was far more vast and powerful than they had ever anticipated.

Rahim wasn't just a warlord; he was a puppet master, with strings that stretched across continents. His influence reached beyond Cairo, his wealth built on a foundation of fear and violence. And while Bijoy and Isabella had made dents in his empire, they hadn't come close to toppling it. They were outnumbered, outgunned, and time was running out.

One evening, after a particularly grueling fight that had left them both bruised and battered, Bijoy and Isabella found themselves hiding in the ruins of an old building. The sound of Rahim's men searching for them echoed through the narrow streets, their footsteps growing closer. Inside the crumbling walls, the tension between Bijoy and Isabella hung in the air, thick and palpable.

"We can't keep doing this," Isabella whispered, her breath coming in short, sharp gasps. Her dark hair was matted with sweat and dirt, her face streaked with blood. Yet even in the dim light, she was beautiful—fierce, determined, and utterly captivating.

Bijoy, leaning against the wall beside her, wiped the blood from his brow. His body ached from the day's battles, but his mind was clear. "We don't have a choice," he replied, his voice low and steady. "As long as Rahim is in power, neither of us will be safe."

Isabella turned to him, her eyes searching his face. "Do you really think we can take him down? He's too powerful, Bijoy. He has resources we can't even begin to imagine."

For a moment, Bijoy was silent. He knew she was right. They had been fighting for weeks, and while they had made progress, it wasn't enough. Rahim's reach was too wide, his forces too strong. But there was something inside Bijoy that refused to give up. He had come to Cairo to bring Isabella to justice, but now, he found himself fighting alongside her, their fates intertwined in a way he hadn't expected.

"I don't know," he admitted, his voice barely above a whisper. "But I do know that we can't stop now. Not until we've given it everything we've got."

Isabella sighed, leaning her head back against the wall. "You're too stubborn for your own good," she said, though there was a softness in her voice that hadn't been there before.

Bijoy glanced at her, a small smile tugging at the corners of his lips. "I could say the same about you."

They sat in silence for a moment, the sounds of the city fading into the background. Outside, Rahim's men were still searching, but for now, they were safe. The ruins provided shelter, a brief respite from the constant danger that surrounded them.

As they sat there, bruised and exhausted, Bijoy found his gaze drifting to Isabella. Over the past few weeks, he had seen her in a new light. She wasn't the same woman he had chased through the rainy streets of Calcutta. She had changed, hardened by the years and the battles she had fought. But beneath that hard exterior, there was still a vulnerability, a part of her that longed for something more than the life she had built.

"You never answered my question," Bijoy said suddenly, breaking the silence.

Isabella raised an eyebrow, her expression cautious. "Which question?"

"Why didn't you run? Back at the Grand Mosque. You could have gotten away. Why didn't you?"

Isabella hesitated, her gaze dropping to the ground. For a long moment, she said nothing. Then, finally, she spoke, her voice quiet and uncertain. "I don't know," she admitted. "Maybe I was tired of running. Or maybe... maybe I wanted you to find me."

Bijoy's heart skipped a beat at her words. There was something raw and honest about the way she said it, something that cut through the walls they had both built around themselves. For the first time since they had reunited, Bijoy saw the woman behind the mask, the woman who had once been torn between two worlds—one of power and one of love.

"Isabella…" Bijoy began, but before he could say more, the sound of approaching footsteps snapped them both back to reality. Rahim's men were getting closer.

They exchanged a glance, the moment between them broken by the harsh reality of their situation. There was no time for confessions, no time for anything but survival.

"We need to move," Bijoy said, his voice firm. Isabella nodded, pushing herself to her feet. They couldn't afford to be caught now, not when they were so close to finding a way out.

Together, they slipped out of the ruins and into the narrow alleyways, the darkness of Cairo closing in around them. They moved quickly and silently, their bodies moving in sync, as if they had been fighting together for years. The connection between them was undeniable, forged in the fires of battle and tempered by the shared weight of their pasts.

As they made their way back to their hideout, Bijoy couldn't shake the feeling that something had shifted between them. There was a closeness now, a bond that had grown stronger with each fight, each narrow escape. And while he still didn't fully trust her, he couldn't deny the feelings that had begun to surface.

They had been ambushed, caught in a deadly trap set by Rahim himself. The fight was brutal, more violent than anything they had faced before. Bijoy had been separated from Isabella in the chaos, and for a moment, he feared the worst. But then, through the smoke and gunfire, he saw her.

Over the next few days, they continued their fight against Rahim's forces. Each victory brought them closer to their goal, but it also made them more aware of the impossibility of their situation. Rahim's network was too vast, his power too great. No matter how many of his men they took down, there were always more to replace them.

It was during one of their last skirmishes that everything changed.

Isabella was fighting for her life, her movements graceful and deadly. She took down one of Rahim's men with a swift kick, but before she could react, another man lunged at her, his knife glinting in the dim light. Without thinking, Bijoy charged forward, his gun blazing. He took down the attacker, saving Isabella once again.

For a moment, they stood there, breathing heavily, their bodies covered in sweat and blood. The world around them faded away, and all that remained was the two of them, standing together in the midst of chaos.

Isabella looked at him, her eyes filled with something he couldn't quite place. Gratitude? Relief? Or maybe something more.

"Thank you," she whispered, her voice barely audible over the sounds of the battle.

Bijoy nodded, his heart racing. "We need to get out of here."

They fought their way out of the ambush, barely escaping with their lives. When they finally reached safety, they collapsed in exhaustion, their bodies aching from the fight. It was then, in the quiet moments after the battle, that the reality of their situation finally hit them.

"We can't keep doing this," Isabella said, her voice filled with frustration. "Rahim is too powerful. We'll never be able to take him down."

Bijoy knew she was right. They had tried everything, but Rahim's grip on Cairo was unbreakable. No matter how hard they fought, they couldn't defeat him alone.

"What do we do?" Bijoy asked, his voice heavy with the weight of their failure.

Isabella hesitated, her eyes meeting his. "We leave. Together."

Bijoy's heart skipped a beat at her words. Leave? After everything they had been through, after all the battles they had fought?

"Are you serious?" he asked, his voice filled with disbelief.

Isabella nodded. "We can't win this fight, Bijoy. Not here. But maybe... maybe we can find peace somewhere else. Away from all of this."

Bijoy stared at her, his mind racing. The thought of leaving Cairo, of abandoning the fight, felt like giving up. But then, as he looked into Isabella's eyes, he realized something. They had been fighting for so long—fighting against Rahim, against each other, against their own pasts. Maybe it was time to stop fighting.

"Where would we go?" he asked quietly.

Isabella smiled, a soft, bittersweet smile. "Back to Calcutta. Where it all began."

Bijoy nodded slowly, the weight of their decision settling over him. They would leave Cairo, leave the smuggling empire behind. Together, they would return to Calcutta, where they hoped to find peace. But even as they made the decision, Bijoy knew that their past would always be a part of them, no matter how far they tried to run.

As they boarded the steamboat back to Calcutta, Bijoy couldn't help but wonder what the future held. Would they finally find the peace they had been searching for? Or would their past come back to haunt them once again? Only time would tell.

As the steamboat cut through the waters, its rhythmic hum filling the night, the distant lights of Calcutta began to shimmer on the horizon. Isabella stood at the railing, her fingers tracing the edge of the medallion that still hung from her neck—the same medallion her mother had given her all those years ago. The wind tugged at her hair, the salt air blending with the faint scent of the city she had once called home.

For a moment, Isabella closed her eyes and let herself drift back in time. She remembered the first time she had made this journey, a young girl stepping off a steamboat with her mother and father into the bustling chaos of Calcutta. The memory was vivid—the warmth of her mother's hand in hers, the stern but protective gaze of her father, and the strange, unfamiliar sounds of a new world opening before her.

But now, everything had changed.

Her mother was gone, her father's legacy had been tainted by crime, and the girl who had once arrived in Calcutta full of hope and innocence had long since disappeared. In her place stood a woman who had seen the darkest sides of life, who had built an empire from the ashes of her father's legacy, only to have it all crumble once again.

Isabella opened her eyes and gazed out at the city. The same city that had once welcomed her now awaited her return, though everything about it felt different. The circle was closing. She had come back to where it all began, but this time, she wasn't the same.

A flicker of movement caught her eye, and she turned to see Bijoy standing a few feet away, watching her. His face was set in that familiar expression of quiet contemplation, his sharp eyes scanning the horizon as if already anticipating the next chapter of their lives.

As their eyes met, Isabella felt a strange sense of peace wash over her. Despite everything they had been through—despite the battles, the betrayals, and the shared wounds—they had survived. And now, they were coming home.

Bijoy stepped closer, his voice low as he spoke, "It feels like a full circle, doesn't it?"

Isabella nodded slowly, the weight of her thoughts pressing down on her. "It does," she whispered, her voice barely audible over the rush of the wind. "But it's not the same. We're not the same."

"No," Bijoy agreed, his eyes never leaving hers. "We're not."

As the shoreline of Calcutta grew clearer, Isabella felt the pull of the city—the memories, the losses, and the new beginnings that awaited them. She wasn't sure if they would find peace here, if their pasts would truly be left behind. But for the first time in a long while, she felt like she had a choice.

The circle may have closed, but a new path was opening.

With a final glance at the approaching shore, Isabella turned back to Bijoy, a soft smile tugging at her lips. "Let's see where this takes us."

And together, they stood at the railing, watching as the shores of Calcutta came into view, knowing that whatever came next, they would face it together.

# Epilogue

The streets of Calcutta were quiet in the early morning mist. The first light of dawn barely touched the rooftops, casting long shadows across the city's narrow lanes. The air was thick with the smell of earth and spice, and a soft breeze stirred the remnants of the previous night's rain.

Bijoy Chatterjee sat on the steps outside his small, modest home, Pluto at his side. The loyal dog, as always, rested his head on Bijoy's lap, his eyes half-closed but alert. Bijoy's cigar smoldered between his fingers, the smoke curling lazily into the air, blending with the fog that clung to the city. He stared out into the distance, lost in thought.

It had been months since they returned from Cairo. The scars of their battles with Rahim al-Zahir had begun to fade, but the memories lingered. They had come back with the promise of peace, but peace, Bijoy had come to realize, was a fleeting thing. He wasn't sure if Calcutta could ever truly be peaceful. The city was too alive, too full of secrets and stories that never ended.

Isabella, too, had changed since their return. The smuggler queen who had ruled the dark corners of Cairo was now a woman seeking a new life, away from the shadows of her past. She had taken refuge in the hills, just outside the city, in a small house surrounded by trees, where the noise and chaos of Calcutta couldn't reach her. It was the quiet she had longed for, far from the life she once led. She no longer carried the weight of her father's empire or the burden of her sins. For the first time, she was free—at least, as free as one could be with a past like hers.

Bijoy visited her often, their lives now entwined in ways neither had expected. They had found something in each other, something neither of them had sought but couldn't deny—a bond forged through survival, respect, and the strangest kind of love. It was fragile, like the city in which they lived, but it was theirs.

As Bijoy sat in the morning light, he thought about the road that had brought them here. From the stormy nights of Calcutta to the scorching heat of Cairo, they had fought battles both with the world and within themselves. And though their journey had been long and fraught with danger, it had led them back here, to the place where it had all begun.

Pluto stirred at his side, his ears perking up as a familiar figure appeared in the distance. Isabella walked toward them, her silhouette barely visible through the mist. She wore a simple sari, her hair loose around her shoulders, the medallion her mother had given her still hanging from her neck, glinting faintly in the early light.

Bijoy smiled as she approached, her footsteps soft and sure. She sat down beside him without a word, her gaze fixed on the horizon where the sun was beginning to rise. They sat in comfortable silence, the weight of the past slowly lifting with each passing moment.

"I never thought I'd be back here," Isabella said quietly, her voice barely above a whisper. "Not like this."

Bijoy took a deep breath, exhaling the last of his cigar smoke. "Neither did I."

They both stared out at the city as it began to wake, its familiar sounds gradually filling the air. For the first time in a long while, the future didn't seem so uncertain. It wasn't without its challenges—there would always be whispers, always be questions about what they had done and where they had been—but they were ready to face it together.

"You think we'll ever truly find peace?" Isabella asked, her voice carrying a note of hope, tempered with realism.

Bijoy smiled faintly, looking at her out of the corner of his eye. "Maybe not. But we'll find something close enough."

Isabella's lips curved into a small smile as she leaned her head against his shoulder, her hand resting lightly on his. "Close enough is all I ever wanted."

The sun rose higher, casting a golden light over the city they had both fought so hard to protect and escape. In that moment, they were no longer Detective Bijoy Chatterjee and the elusive smuggler Isabella Rossi. They were just two people who had finally found their way back to where they belonged.

Together.

As the day unfolded, so too did their future—unknown, unpredictable, but theirs to live, side by side. And in that, they found peace.

**Biswajit Paria** crafts captivating stories that merge history, intrigue, and the nuances of human connections. His love for crime fiction and period dramas is vividly expressed in *The Silent Messenger*, where he skillfully weaves a tale of romance, deception, and self-discovery set against the dynamic landscapes of Calcutta, Venice, and Cairo.

With a foundation in literature and the arts, Biswajit delves into the complexities of life's moral challenges, exploring themes like loyalty, ambition, and redemption. His narratives are shaped by colonial legacies and personal dilemmas, creating immersive experiences that keep readers engaged while provoking deep reflection.